Dear Parent:
Your child's love of reading starts here!

Every child learns in a different way and at his or her own speed. Some go back and forth between reading levels and read favorite books again and again. Others read through each level in order. You can help your young reader improve and become more confident by encouraging his or her own interests and abilities. From books your child reads with you to the first books he or she reads alone, there are I Can Read Books for every stage of reading:

SHARED READING
Basic language, word repetition, and whimsical illustrations, ideal for sharing with your emergent reader

BEGINNING READING
Short sentences, familiar words, and simple concepts for children eager to read on their own

READING WITH HELP
Engaging stories, longer sentences, and language play for developing readers

READING ALONE
Complex plots, challenging vocabulary, and high-interest topics for the independent reader

ADVANCED READING
Short paragraphs, chapters, and exciting themes for the perfect bridge to chapter books

I Can Read Books have introduced children to the joy of reading since 1957. Featuring award-winning authors and illustrators and a fabulous cast of beloved characters, I Can Read Books set the standard for beginning readers.

A lifetime of discovery begins with the magical words
"I Can Read!"

Visit www.icanread.com for information
on enriching your child's reading experience.

3 3113 03085 6548

Library of Congress catalog card number: 2005017662
ISBN-10: 0-06-058354-1 (pbk.) — ISBN-13: 978-0-06-058354-5 (pbk.)
ISBN-10: 0-06-058353-3 (trade bdg.) — ISBN-13: 978-0-06-058353-8 (trade bdg.)

11   12   13   14   SCP   10   9   8   7   6   ❖   First Edition

I Can Read!

BEGINNING 1 READING

The Berenstain Bears
Out West

Stan & Jan Berenstain

HarperCollins*Publishers*

"Come. It's time to leave
for our ranch vacation."

"But, Papa, this isn't the way to the train station."

"We can't visit
Uncle Tex by train.
His ranch is far.
We must go by plane."

"Wow! Wait 'til we tell
Cousin Fred.
Look! There's the airport
just ahead."

"Fasten your seat belts.
We're ready to fly."

"We're above the clouds!
We're high in the sky!

"Look! Rivers and forests
down below!
On the tops of the mountains,
caps of snow!"

"Wake up! Wake up,
Papa Bear!
The pilot says
we're almost there."

PLEASE STAY IN YOUR SEATS.
DO NOT STAND.
WE ARE ABOUT
TO LAND.

"There's Uncle Tex
over there.
As you can see,
he's a cowboy bear.

"Just take a look
at how he's dressed
in a ten-gallon hat,
chaps and vest,
cowboy boots,
and all the rest."

"Welcome folks,
to the glorious West!

"I've got the finest ranch
you've ever seen,
from the Rio Grande
to Abilene.

"We've got horses, cattle, a barn, of course.

This is Red, my favorite horse."

"May we ride him?"

"Hmm, that might be risky.
Red can be a little frisky.

"Cubs, I have ponies
for you to ride.

"But first, meet Aunt Min,
my lovely bride."

"Tex, I think I
can handle Red."

"Red is frisky, as I said.
But be my guest.
You go to it."

"No, Papa! No!
Do not do it!"

"Will you please
relax, my dear?
There is not
a thing to fear.
And may I please
remind you all
no horse on Earth
can make me fall."

"You must be a little
out of practice.
Er, sorry about
that giant cactus.

"Your ponies, cubs.
Climb on, Sister.
You, too, lad.

"And here's a buggy
for baby, mom, and dad.

"This way, folks.
Follow me.
The glorious West
has lots to see.

"Canyons,

cliffs,

rivers,

ridges,

the Painted Desert,

natural bridges.

"Now think of the things
that are no longer here—
the hopes and dreams
of yesteryear.

"And if you use
your mind's eye,
you can almost see them
in the sky.

"Pony Express riders
brave and bold,

folks who came west
to pan for gold,

great bison herds
and wagon trains

that reached across
the western plains.

"Folks, I do not like
to break the spell,
but I think I smell
a special smell.

   "*Mmm! Mmm!*
   Yes, it's true!
   I smell Aunt Min's
   barbecue."

So back they went
with Uncle Tex
to a beefsteak dinner
at the B-Bar-X.

After dinner
they watched the night sky
and listened to
the coyote's cry.

Then it was time
to leave the West:

Uncle Tex, Aunt Min,
and all the rest.

There were bear hugs
and kisses all around.
Then they were up and away . . .

and homeward bound.

LAKE COUNTY PUBLIC LIBRARY
INDIANA

Some materials may be renewed by phone, in person, or through the online catalog
if there are no reserves or fines due.

www.lcplin.org   LibraryLine: (219) 756-9356